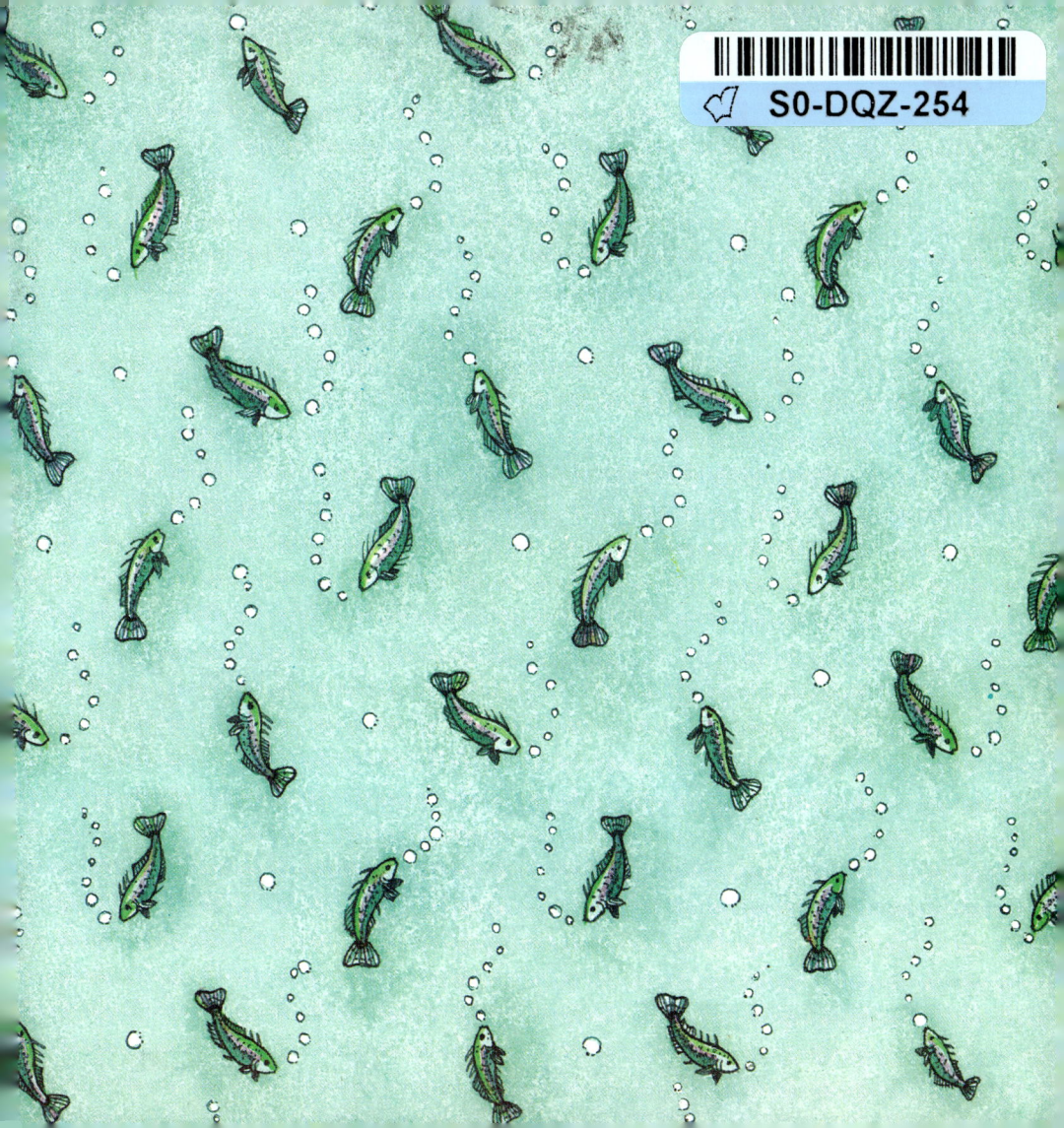

This book is dedicated to
my grandmother, Margaret Glover,
with love, respect, and admiration.

Copyright © 1990 by Naomi Russell
American text prepared by Rebecca Kalusky

All rights reserved.

CIP Data is available.

First published in the United States 1991 by
Dutton Children's Books,
a division of Penguin Books USA Inc.

Originally published in Great Britain 1990 by
Methuen Children's Books,
Michelin House, 81 Fulham Road, London SW3 6RB

Printed in Singapore
First American Edition   10 9 8 7 6 5 4 3 2 1
ISBN 0-525-44729-6

The Stream

by NAOMI RUSSELL

DUTTON CHILDREN'S BOOKS
NEW YORK

Over the mountains the clouds grew dark. Soon rain poured down over the hills and mountains. The water soaked into the earth, deeper and deeper. At last the water reached solid stone and could travel down no more.

More rain fell, and the underground water began rising. It forced its way up through cracks in the ground—and a little mountain spring was born. Later, when warmer weather came, the snow high in the mountains began to melt. Down flowed the water, into the spring. The spring grew bigger. Animals came there to drink and swim.

Over time, more rain and more melted snow made the spring grow. It flowed over its banks and trickled down the mountain in a stream. More animals came to live along the stream's shores and in its clear water.

Water from other springs joined the stream and made it bigger. Sometimes it filled deep pools where fish swam. When the stream ran down steep places, it flowed fast. When it fell down over rocks—*whoosh*—it became a tumbling waterfall!

The stream rushed into a valley where a river flowed. Into the river poured the stream. The river was wide and slow. It ambled through woods and fields and under bridges. It passed villages and towns and cities.

Open ↓

People came to the river to fish and boat and swim. With a kick of his flipper, under the water went a diver. Among the fish and eels, he found secrets hidden in the riverbed.

Some river water was sent through pipes to a pond in the park. In the summer, swans lived there. In winter the water froze. Children skated on the ice.

Some of the water from the river flowed into a kind of lake that people had made, called a reservoir. Birds nested there in tall reeds.

Some of the water was piped from the reservoir to businesses and factories...

to zoos... and to houses.

Some water was used for washing cars...

Open ↓

and some for washing people! They drank it, cooked with it, and used it in their gardens. In certain places, the water that went back into the river was dirty. In other places, the water was treated so it was clean before it went into the river.

On and on the river flowed, hundreds of miles from where it had begun as a tiny mountain spring. It had traveled through meadows and marshes, along hills and between cliffs. At last the river came to a sandy beach and flowed right into...

Meanwhile, high in the mountains, a dry season had begun. Not enough rain fell. The mountain spring became muddy. There was less and less room for frogs to splash and fish to swim. But far away, over the sea, something else was happening....

Some of the seawater formed into tiny droplets that rose into the air. The droplets rose higher and higher and crowded together to form clouds. The wind blew the clouds over the land. The clouds grew darker. And then ...

it rained again! A few drops fell at first, then more and more. It rained on forests and farms, on city sidewalks, on homes and schools, and on people. It rained on hills and mountains.

Some of the rain fell into the thirsty mountain spring. The water rose higher, clear and sparkling, and its trip went on as before. The spring splashed down into the stream. The stream ran into the river. The river flowed past farms and cities on its long, long trip to the sea.